WITHDRAWN

Crocodile Gene
and his friends

by Eduard Uspensky
illustrations by Vladimir Shpitalnik

Translated by Nina Ignatowicz

Alfred A. Knopf • New York

THIS IS A BORZOI BOOK PUBLISHED BY ALFRED A. KNOPF, INC.

Text copyright © 1989 by Eduard Uspensky
Illustrations copyright © 1994 by Vladimir Shpitalnik
Translation copyright © 1994 by Nina Ignatowicz

Book design by Mina Greenstein
Manufactured in the United States of America
10 9 8 7 6 5 4 3 2 1

Library of Congress Cataloging-in-Publication Data
Uspenskii, E. (Eduard)
[Krokodil Gena i ego druz'ia. English]
Crocodile Gene and his friends : a story / by Eduard Uspensky ;
translated from the Russian by Nina Ignatowicz ; illustrated by Vladimir Shpitalnik.
p.   cm.
Summary: A small animal, unknown to science, moves to the city, meets a
crocodile and a young girl, and together they help others who are looking for friends.
ISBN 0-679-82062-0 (trade)
[1. Friendship—Fiction. 2. Animals—Fiction.] I. Ignatowicz, Nina
II. Shpitalnik, Vladimir, ill. III. Title.
PZ7.U696Cr 1994 94-13357

Author's Note

Dear American boys and girls,

Twenty-five years ago I wrote a book for Russian boys and girls about a little animal named Floptop. Then recently I visited my friends in your country and learned that you have a completely different way of life, and so you may not understand some things in this book. For instance, why does Floptop live in a telephone booth? It's not because he likes to talk on the phone, but because people in Russia have a very hard time finding places to live. There aren't enough apartments and houses for everyone.

And it's not only apartments; we also don't have enough things in the stores for everyone. Often we have to stand in long lines for sausages, jackets, televisions, and even light bulbs.

But I'll tell you what we've always had a lot of in our country, and that's *bosses*. And these bosses would pretend that they were working very hard when, in fact, all they were doing was putting out schedules and rules, forbidding this, permitting that, ordering this, denying that.

But of course my book isn't only about bosses and long lines. It's about some happy and very honest friends: Gene the crocodile, a little girl named Gail, and funny Floptop. And if you happen to come across anything in my book that's hard to understand, don't be surprised. That's how things once were in Russia. Nowadays everything is changing quickly, and for the better.

EDUARD USPENSKY

Introduction,

Which You Don't
Have to Read
Unless You Feel Like It

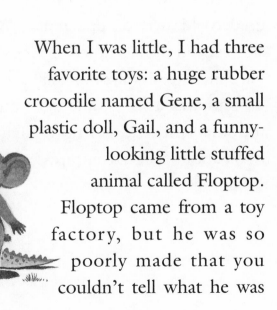

When I was little, I had three favorite toys: a huge rubber crocodile named Gene, a small plastic doll, Gail, and a funny-looking little stuffed animal called Floptop. Floptop came from a toy factory, but he was so poorly made that you couldn't tell what he was

was supposed to be—a rabbit, a dog, a cat, or an Australian kangaroo. His eyes were big and yellow like an owl's, his head was round like a rabbit's head, and his tail was short and fluffy, just like a baby bear's. He was little, exactly the right size to sit in my lap.

My parents claimed that Floptop was an animal unknown to science who lived in hot tropical forests.

At first I was so afraid of Floptop that I didn't want to be left alone with him. But gradually I got used to his weird appearance. We became friends, and I loved him as much as Gene, my rubber crocodile, and my plastic doll, Gail.

This was a long time ago, but I still remember my small friends, and now I have written a whole book about their adventures.

chapter 1

EEP IN A TROPI-
CAL forest there once
lived a funny-looking
little creature named
Floptop. Actually, he wasn't called anything while
he lived in his tropical forest. He was named
Floptop later, when he left the forest and met
humans. It's only people who give names to animals. It's people who told the elephant that he was

an elephant, the giraffe that she was a giraffe, and the rabbits that they were rabbits. And so the little creature never gave a thought to what he was called, he just lived, and he lived in a faraway tropical forest.

Early one morning, Floptop woke up, crossed his paws behind his back, and set out for a leisurely walk to get some fresh air. As he was strolling past a large fruit orchard he noticed several crates filled with oranges. Without another thought he climbed inside one of the crates and started to eat breakfast. He ate two whole oranges and was so stuffed that he lay down on top of the fruit and fell asleep.

Floptop slept so soundly that he didn't even hear when workers came and nailed down the tops of all the crates. Then they loaded the crates onto a ship and sent them off on a journey.

The crates sailed the seas and oceans for a long time, finally landing in a fruit store in a very large city. When the crates were opened, one had almost no oranges inside, only a very fat Floptop.

The salesclerks dragged Floptop out of his cabin

and sat him down on a table. But Floptop could not sit. He had been inside the crate too long and his paws had gone numb. He looked around him. Then suddenly he flopped down from the table onto a chair. But he didn't stay long on the chair, either. Soon he flopped down again—onto the floor.

"Look at him! What a floptop!" said the store manager. "He can't sit still!"

This is how the little creature found out that his name was Floptop.

"But what am I going to do with you?" asked the manager. "I can't sell you."

"I don't know," answered Floptop. "Do as you wish."

The manager tucked Floptop under his arm and took him to the city zoo.

But the zoo didn't want Floptop. It was overcrowded, and furthermore, Floptop was a creature completely unknown to science. Nobody knew whether to put him with the rabbits, the tigers, or the sea turtles.

So the store manager tucked Floptop under his

arm again and took him to meet his cousin, the manager of a thrift shop.

"You know what?" said his cousin. "I like this little creature. He looks like a rejected toy. I'll offer him a job. Will you work for me?"

"Yes," answered Floptop, "but what will I have to do?"

"You will stand in the store window and attract the attention of passersby. Agreed?"

"Agreed," said the little creature. "And where will I live?"

"Live? How about here?" The manager pointed to an old telephone booth standing by the store's entrance. "This will be your home!"

That's how Floptop came to work in a big store and live in his small house. It wasn't the best house in town, but Floptop had the telephone right by him, and he could call anyone he wanted to without ever leaving home.

The fact that he didn't know anyone to call yet didn't bother him in the least.

chapter 2

IN THE SAME CITY where Floptop landed there lived a crocodile by the name of Gene. Every morning he would wake up in his small apartment, wash himself, eat his breakfast, and head for the zoo where he worked...as a crocodile.

At the zoo Gene would take off his clothes, hang his suit, hat, and cane on a nail and lie down in the sun by the pool. On his cage hung a sign that said:

AFRICAN CROCODILE
Name: Gene
Age: Fifty Years
Feeding and Petting Are Allowed

At the end of every workday Gene would put on his clothes and walk back to his small apartment. At home he would read the newspaper, smoke a pipe, and for the rest of the evening he would play tick-tack-toe with himself.

One evening he lost forty games in a row to himself.

"Why am I always alone?" he said. "I need friends."

He took a pencil and wrote the following notice:

A Young Cracadile Fifty Years Old
Wants to Acquire Friends.
All Interested Come to
Grand Pastry Street, House Number 15, Bloc 7.
Ring Three and a Half Times.

That same evening he hung copies of the notice all around the city. Then he returned home to wait.

chapter 3

ATE IN THE EVENING of the following day someone rang Gene's doorbell. On the threshold stood a slender, very serious-looking little girl.

"Your notice has three errors," she said.

"That's impossible!" exclaimed Gene. He thought he had made at least eighteen. "Which ones?"

"Well, the word 'crocodile' is spelled with two

o's, and also, how can you say you're young when you are fifty years old?"

"That's because crocodiles live for three hundred years. That means I am very young," objected Gene.

"You should still spell right. Anyway, my name is Gail. I work in the children's theater."

"And my name is Gene. I work at the zoo. As a crocodile."

Just then the doorbell rang again.

"Who's there?" asked the crocodile.

"It's me, Floptop!" said the strange-looking creature who entered the room. He was tiny and brown, with big bulging eyes and a short fluffy tail.

"Who are you?" Gene asked him.

"I don't know," answered the guest.

"You really truly don't know?" asked the girl.

"Really truly."

"Are you by any chance a bear cub?"

"I don't know," said Floptop. "I could be a bear cub."

"No," said the crocodile, "he doesn't look even a little bit like a bear cub. Bears have small eyes. Look at the size of his eyes!"

"Then maybe he is a puppy," said Gail.

"Maybe," agreed Floptop. "Do puppies climb trees?"

"No, they don't climb trees," answered Gene. "They bark."

"How?"

"Like this: Arf, arf!" barked the crocodile.

"No, I don't know how to do that," Floptop said sadly. "I guess that means I'm not a puppy!"

"Oh, I know who you are," said Gail. "You are probably a leopard."

"Probably," agreed Floptop. "I am probably a leopard!"

Since neither of them had ever seen a leopard, they stepped away from him. Just in case.

"Let's look it up in the dictionary," suggested Gail. "All the words are explained there, beginning with every letter."

"Fine," agreed Floptop. "Which letter are we going to look up?"

"The letter *R*," said Gail, "because leopards *r-r-roar*."

"And the letter *B*," Gene added, "because leopards *b-b-bite*."

"But since I don't roar and I don't bite," said Floptop, "that means I am not a leopard!

"What if you don't find out who I am? Does that mean you won't want to be friends with me?"

"Of course not!" answered Gene. "It all depends on you. If you prove to be a good friend, we will be happy to be your friends. Am I right?" he asked the little girl.

"Absolutely!" agreed Gail. "We will be very happy!"

"Hooray!" shouted Floptop. "Hooray!" And he jumped as high as the ceiling.

chapter 4

SOON GENE, GAIL, AND Floptop were spending almost every evening together. After work they gathered at the crocodile's home and talked, drank coffee, and played tick-tack-toe. And still Floptop couldn't believe he had found some true friends.

What, he wondered one day, if I invited Gene to visit me? Would he come? Of course he would come, Floptop reassured himself. After all, we are friends! But what if Gene says no?

Quickly, so he wouldn't have time to change his mind, Floptop picked up the phone and called the crocodile.

"Hello, Gene, this is Floptop!" he said. "Are you doing anything special?"

"Not really," answered the crocodile.

"You know what? Why don't you come over?"

"To your house?" asked Gene, surprised. "What for?"

"To drink coffee," said Floptop. That was the first thing that had come into his head.

"Well, why not?" said the crocodile. "I will be happy to come."

"Hooray!" Floptop almost shouted. But then he thought, There is nothing unusual about one friend visiting another. And instead of shouting "Hooray," I should think of how to make him most welcome. He said to the crocodile, "By the way, would you please bring along some cups? I don't seem to have any."

"Very well, I will bring them. Good-bye."

Gene began to get ready to leave. But Floptop called again.

"You know what? I don't seem to have a coffeepot, either. Would you mind bringing yours?"

"Very well, I will bring that too."

"And there's just one other tiny thing," said Floptop. "On your way over, would you stop and buy some coffee? I seem to have run out of it."

Gene was all ready to leave when Floptop called again and asked Gene to bring a small bucket.

"A small bucket? What on earth for?"

"Well, you see, on your way here you will pass a water fountain, and if you would get some water, I won't have to leave the house."

"Very well," agreed Gene. "I will bring all the things you asked for."

A short time later he arrived on Floptop's doorstep, loaded up like a porter at a railroad station.

"I am so glad you could come," his host greeted him. "But I have a confession. I don't know how to make coffee. I have never even tried. Would you mind making it?"

Gene got to work. He gathered some wood, lit a small bonfire near the telephone booth, and put the

coffeepot on top of the fire. Half an hour later the coffee was ready. Floptop was very happy.

"Well, what do you think? Wasn't I a good host?" Floptop asked the crocodile when he was getting ready to leave.

"The coffee was excellent," answered Gene. "But I must ask you a favor. The next time you'd like to see me, don't be bashful, come to my house. And tell me what you would like me to serve — tea, coffee, or supper. I have everything at home. It will be much easier for me that way. Agreed?"

"Agreed," said Floptop. He was a little upset that Gene had admonished him. Still, he was very happy. After all, the crocodile himself had paid him a visit.

chapter 5

THE NEXT EVENING Floptop was the first to arrive at the crocodile's house. Gene was reading. He loved to read thick, serious books: dictionaries, textbooks, phone books.

"Where's Gail?" asked Floptop.

"She promised to come by tonight," answered Gene. "I don't know what's keeping her."

"Let's visit her then," said Floptop. "After all, friends should visit each other."

"Let's go," agreed the crocodile.

They found Gail at home. She was lying on her bed crying.

"I am sick," she told her friends. "I have a fever. Because of me there won't be a performance at the children's theater tonight. The children will come, and I won't be there!"

"There *will* be a performance!" the crocodile announced grandly. "I will take over for you."

"You will? That would be wonderful! Tonight we are putting on *Little Red Riding Hood,* and I play the part of Red Riding Hood. Do you know the story?"

"Of course I know it!"

"Fantastic! If you're good, nobody will even notice the switch. Talent works wonders!" And she gave the crocodile her little red hood.

When the children arrived at the theater later that night, they saw a very unusual performance. Gene came onstage wearing a red hood. As he strolled across the stage he sang:

"Promenading down the aisle
was a huge big crocodile…"

A gray wolf came up to him.

"Hello, Little Red Riding Hood," he said in a stiff voice. Then he looked at the audience and froze in his tracks.

"Hello," answered the crocodile.

"Where are you going?"

"Nowhere, really. I'm just taking a walk."

"Are you on your way to visit your grandmother, perhaps?"

"Yes, of course." The crocodile suddenly remembered. "I'm on my way to visit my grandmother."

"And where does your grandmother live?"

"Grandmother? In Africa, on the banks of the Nile."

"And I was sure your grandmother lived over

there, in the hut at the edge of the forest."

"You are absolutely right! I have a grandmother who lives there, too. I was about to pay her a visit."

"Good!" said the wolf. Then he ran to the hut, ate Little Red Riding Hood's grandmother, and got into her bed.

Meanwhile, Gene had left the stage. He sat backstage and reread the story. At last he appeared at the grandmother's hut.

He knocked at the door. "Hello! Who here is my grandmother?"

"Hello!" answered the wolf. "I'm your grandmother."

"Why do you have such big ears, Grandmother?" asked the crocodile, this time remembering his lines.

"To hear you better with, my dear."

"But why are you so shaggy, Grandmother?"

"I didn't have time to shave, Granddaughter. I have been so busy..." The wolf jumped out of the bed. "Now I'm going to eat you up!"

"Well! We will see about that!" said the crocodile, and he pounced on the gray wolf. He had completely forgotten where he was and what his role was.

The gray wolf ran off the stage. The children were delighted. They had never seen such an interesting *Little Red Riding Hood* before. They clapped for the longest time, begging to see the play again. But for some reason the crocodile refused. And for some reason he begged Floptop not to tell Gail about his performance.

chapter 6

GAIL WAS SICK for many days, and the doctor wouldn't allow any visitors, for fear that her friends would catch her illness. Gene and Floptop had only each other for company.

One evening after work, Floptop decided to stop by the zoo and visit the crocodile.

He was almost at the zoo when he noticed a mangy-looking dog sitting in the street, whimpering.

"Why are you howling?" asked Floptop.

"I'm not howling," answered the dog. "I'm crying."

"Why are you crying, then?"

But the dog continued to cry pitifully and wouldn't say anything more.

Floptop sat down next to the dog, waited until she'd had a good cry, then ordered, "Okay, spill it out! What happened to you?"

"She threw me out of the house."

"Who threw you out?"

"My owner!" The dog started to sob again.

"For what?" asked Floptop.

"She just did. For I don't know what."

"And what is your name?"

"Toby." The dog calmed down and told Floptop her short, sad tale.

Here it is:

THE SHORT AND SAD TALE
OF THE LITTLE DOG TOBY

Toby was a tiny puppy when she was brought to her new owner.

"Oh, isn't she cute!" her owner kept repeating, showing her off to her friends. "Isn't she adorable!"

All her friends agreed that she was cute and adorable. They played with the puppy and gave her treats.

Time passed, and the puppy grew. Now she was no longer cute and adorable. Now when her owner showed her to guests, she never said, "Oh, isn't she adorable!" but the opposite: "My dog is so ugly! But I don't have the heart to throw her out. I have such a kind heart. If I did throw her out, my heart would shatter to pieces in five minutes from grief!"

But one day someone brought her a new puppy. He was as cute and adorable as Toby had been.

Without another thought, the owner threw Toby out the door. And her heart didn't shatter into tiny pieces in five minutes, or six minutes, or even ninety-eight. After all, she couldn't keep two animals!

THE END

28

What am I going to do with this dog? thought Floptop.

He could, of course, take her with him. But Floptop wasn't sure how his friends would feel about that. What if they didn't like dogs? He could leave Toby on the street, but he felt sorry for her. What if she caught a cold?

"You know what?" Floptop said finally. "Here's my key. Go to my house and rest. Later we'll think of something."

And he headed for the zoo.

chapter 7

AT THE ZOO'S entrance Floptop ran into Gail.

"Hooray!" cried Floptop. "You're well again!"

"Yes," answered Gail, "I'm allowed to go out now."

"I think you've lost a little weight," said Floptop.

"Is it very noticeable?" asked Gail.

"No!" Floptop replied. "It's just barely noticeable. You've lost just a *little* bit of weight. So little, so little, that you have even gained a little!"

That made Gail happy, and together the friends walked into the zoo.

Gene, as always, was lying in the sun reading a book.

"Look at him," Gail said to Floptop. "I never realized he was so fat!"

"You're right," Floptop agreed. "He is almost obese! He looks like a hot dog with paws!"

"Hello, Gene!" Floptop shouted to the crocodile.

"I am not Gene," answered the crocodile, offended. "I am Val. I work the second shift. Your friend Gene is getting dressed. He will be out in a minute." The fat crocodile turned his back to them in a huff.

Just then Gene came out wearing his elegant coat and beautiful hat.

"Hello," he said, smiling. "Shall we go to my house?"

"Yes!" agreed Gail and Floptop. They liked visiting the crocodile.

At Gene's house the three friends drank coffee, talked, and played different kinds of board games. All evening Floptop tried to tell them about the dog, but he never found the right moment.

Suddenly there was a knock on the door.

"Come in!" said Gene.

A huge lion wearing a hat and glasses entered the room.

"Lion Chander, at your service," he introduced himself.

The three friends bowed low to the lion and edged as far away from him as they could.

"Tell me, please," asked Chander, "is this the residence of the crocodile who advertised for friends?"

"Yes, it is," Gene answered. "He does live here, but he doesn't need friends anymore. He already has friends."

"I am very sorry to hear that!" The lion gave a deep sigh and turned to leave. "Good-bye."

"Wait!" Floptop cried. "What kind of friend are you looking for?"

"I'm not sure," answered the lion. "Just a friend, that's all."

"I think I can help you," said Floptop. "Sit down and wait a few minutes while I run home. Okay?"

In a little while Floptop was back, leading Toby on a leash.

"This is who I had in mind," he said. "I have a feeling you'll be just right for each other!"

"But this is a very small dog," said the lion, "and I am very big!"

"That's just it!" said Floptop. "You'll protect her."

"You are right," agreed Chander. "What can you do?" he asked Toby.

"Nothing," answered Toby.

"In my opinion that's good, too," Gail told the lion. "You will be able to teach her anything you want!"

They may be right, Chander decided. "In that

case," he said to Toby, "I will be happy to be your friend. How about you?"

"Me too!" Toby wagged her tail. "I will try my best to be a good friend."

The new friends thanked Floptop, Gene, and Gail and said good-bye.

"Well done!" Gail praised Floptop when they had left. "You did the right thing."

"It was nothing," said Floptop, embarrassed. "It's not worth talking about."

"Do you realize," Gail said suddenly, "how many lonely Tobys and Chanders there are in our city?"

"How many?" asked Floptop.

"Many!" answered the little girl. "They don't have any friends at all. Nobody comes to their birthday parties. And there's no one to comfort them when they are sad."

As Gene listened a large, clear teardrop slowly rolled out of one eye. Looking at him, Floptop also felt like crying, but his teardrop was so tiny that he felt embarrassed.

"There must be something we can do for them!" exclaimed the crocodile. "I want to help them!"

"I want to help too," said Floptop, "but how?"

"Very simple," said Gail. "We have to get them all together and introduce them to one another."

"How are we going to do that?" asked Floptop.

"I don't know," said Gail.

"I do!" announced Gene. "We will post notices telling them to come to us. And when they come, we will introduce them to one another."

The three friends liked the idea and decided to hand out notices all over the city. They would try to find a friend for everyone who came to them. And they would turn the house where the crocodile lived into the House of Friendship.

"And so," said Gene, "tomorrow we begin our work!"

chapter 8

THE FOLLOWING EVENING the work was in full swing. Gene, as the chief authority on writing notices, sat at the table and wrote:

THE OPENING OF HOUSE OF FRIENDSHIP:
ANYONE WHO WANTS A FRIEND,
COME TO US!

Floptop ran outside with the notices. He tacked them up everywhere: on walls of houses, on fences, even on passing horses.

Meanwhile, Gail cleaned the house. Then she placed a chair in the middle of the room and hung a sign on its back:

FOR VISITORS

At last the three friends sat down on the couch to rest.

Suddenly the front door gave a tiny squeak and a shifty-eyed old woman darted into the room leading a big gray rat on a rope.

Gail screamed and jumped up on the couch. Gene shot out of his seat, ran into the closet, and slammed the door behind him. Only Floptop remained sitting calmly on the couch. He had never

seen a rat before, so he didn't know he had to be afraid of them.

"Laura! Go to your place!" ordered the old woman.

The rat quickly scrambled into the woman's handbag, so that only a cunning little head with long whiskers and black beady eyes was visible.

Gradually everyone calmed down. Gail sat on the couch again, and Gene emerged from the closet wearing a new tie.

In the meantime the little old woman had sat on the chair with the FOR VISITORS sign. "Which one of you is the crocodile?" she asked.

"I am," answered Gene, straightening his tie.

"That is good," said the little old woman, and fell silent.

"What is good?" asked Gene.

"It's good that you are green and flat."

"And why is it good that I am green and flat?"

"Because if you lie down on the lawn, nobody will see you."

"And why should I lie down on the lawn?" asked the crocodile.

"You'll find out later."

"Who are you," Gail asked finally, "and what do you do?"

"My name is Fedora," answered the old woman, "and I go around looking for evil."

"Do you mean evil deeds?" Gail asked. "But why?"

"What do you mean, why? I want to be famous."

"But isn't it better to do good deeds?" asked Gene.

"No," answered the old woman. "You don't get famous doing good deeds. I do five evil deeds a day. I need assistants."

"What kinds of deeds?"

"All kinds," said the old woman. "I shoot at pigeons with a slingshot. Pour water from my window onto passersby. And I always, *always* cross the street where you're not supposed to."

"That's all good and fine," exclaimed the crocodile, "but why must I lie on the lawn?"

"Very simple," explained Fedora. "You lie on the lawn, and because you are green, nobody can see you. We tie a string around a wallet and we toss it on the sidewalk. When a passerby stoops down to pick it up, we yank the wallet from under his nose! Isn't that a great idea?"

"No," said Gene, offended. "I don't like it one bit! Besides, you can catch a cold lying on the lawn."

"I'm afraid that we don't see eye to eye," Gail told the visitor. "Our intentions are just the opposite—we want to do good deeds. We have even organized a house of friendship!"

"What!" shrieked the old woman. "House of Friendship! I am declaring war on you. Good-bye!"

"Wait!" The crocodile stopped her. "Do you care about who you declare war on?"

"Not really."

"In that case, don't declare it on us. We are much too busy for that. Find someone else!"

"It doesn't matter to me. I can declare war on someone else," said the old woman. "It's no skin off my nose. Laura, forward march!" she ordered. The rat scrambled out of Fedora's handbag, and they both disappeared through the door.

chapter 9

THE NEXT EVENING it was Gail's turn to welcome guests to the House of Friendship. Gene and Floptop sat in the corner of the room playing lotto.

The doorbell rang sharply and a boy appeared on the threshold. He would have looked like any ordinary boy if he weren't so untidy and grubby.

"Is this where you give out friends?" he asked without a greeting.

"We don't give, we match," Gail corrected him.

"What's the difference? The important thing is, is it here or not?"

"Here, here," the girl reassured him.

"And what kind of friend do you want?" asked the crocodile.

"I want, I want…" said the boy, and his eyes began to shine. "I need…a failer."

"What kind of failer?"

"Someone who gets nothing but F's in school."

"Why do you want someone who gets only F's?"

"What do you mean, why? Because the next time my mother tells me, 'You've gotten six F's again!' I can answer her, 'Big deal, six! One of my friends got eight!' Get it?"

"I get it," said the crocodile. "And would you like him to be a bully, too?"

"What for?" asked the boy.

"What for? So when you come home and your mother tells you, 'You've got a bump on your head again!' you could answer, 'Big deal, it's only one bump! You should've seen a friend of mine. He's got four bumps!'"

"You're right!" shouted the boy happily, looking at the crocodile with new respect. "And he should be good with a slingshot. So when I'm told, 'You've broken someone's window again,' I could say, 'Big deal, one window! A friend of mine broke two windows!' Right?"

"You are right," Gene agreed.

"He must also have good manners."

"Why?" asked Gail.

"What do you mean, why? My mother doesn't allow me to be friends with rude children."

"Oh, dear," said Gail. "If I understand you correctly, you are looking for a friend who has good manners, gets failing grades, and is a bully."

"Exactly," agreed the boy.

"In that case, come see us again tomorrow. We'll do our best to find someone for you."

With his head held high, the grubby visitor left. Needless to say, he didn't bid them good-bye.

"What are we going to do?" asked Gail. "I don't think we should try to find him a bully. I think we should find him someone nice, someone he can learn from."

"I don't agree," said Gene. "We have to find him what he wants. Otherwise we would be cheating. And I was not brought up that way."

"You're absolutely right," agreed Floptop. "We have to find him what he wants."

"Oh, very well," agreed Gail. "And which of you is going to take care of this?"

"I will!" declared Floptop. He liked difficult tasks.

"And so will I!" said the crocodile. He simply wanted to help Floptop.

chapter 10

THE NEXT DAY THE two friends were walking slowly down the street when suddenly they heard a *b-b-boom!* Something struck the crocodile painfully on his head.

"Was it you?" Gene asked Floptop.

"Was I what?"

"Was it you who hit me?"

"No!" Floptop answered. "I didn't hit anyone!"

Just then they heard the *b-b-boom!* again, and something struck Floptop very painfully.

"You see," he said, "someone hit me too!" Floptop looked around him and noticed a very familiar gray rat sitting on top of a fence post.

"Look!" he told the crocodile. "It's Fedora's rat! Now I know who's attacking us!"

Floptop proved to be right. It was indeed the old Fedora.

She had been taking a walk with her pet rat, Laura, when she caught sight of Gene and Floptop. The two friends looked so happy that she wanted to do something nasty to spoil their mood. Fedora grabbed Laura and ran ahead of Gene and Floptop. Then she hid behind the fence.

When the two friends came closer, she took a large piece of paper out of her handbag and quickly crumpled it into a ball. Then she tied an elastic string around it. Holding one end of the string, she hurled the ball at them. After the ball hit Gene on the head, it bounced back to Fedora, who quickly threw it at her other target.

The next time the ball appeared Gene turned quickly and caught it in his teeth. Then he and Floptop slowly started to cross the street. The elastic string around the ball kept stretching and stretching.

When Fedora sneaked out of her hiding place to look for her ball, Floptop shouted "Fire!" and Gene unclenched his teeth.

With the speed of a bullet, the ball flew back across the street and struck its owner—hard. The old woman was blown over the fence as if she'd been struck by a tornado.

When she finally managed to get back on her feet, she was ten times as mad as she had been before. "Scoundrels! Hooligans! You miserable scum!" she wanted to shout. But she couldn't because the paper ball was stuck in her mouth.

The furious Fedora tried to spit out the ball, but it wouldn't spit out. The ball was stuck!

What should she do? She ran to the hospital to see the famous doctor Ivanov.

"Shoo, bloo, phew," she said, her words garbled by the paper ball.

"Shoe, shoe, what?" asked the doctor.

"Shoo, phew, shoo!"

"No," he answered, "I don't sell shoes."

The old woman shook her head furiously.

"Not shoo, shoo, shoo! Poo!"

"I can't understand a word you're saying!" shouted Ivanov, and shoved Fedora out the door.

For the rest of the evening Fedora could only mumble and grumble and could not utter one single word. But so many curse words collected in her mouth that when the ball finally became soggy enough to spit out, this is what spilled out with it:

"Scoundrelshooligansillshowyouathingortwo yougreencrocodileyoumiserablegreencrocodile."

And that wasn't all! Some of the curse words she swallowed, together with the elastic string.

chapter 11

THE DAY AFTER their adventure with Fedora, Gene and Floptop went around to all the schools, asking the school guards if they knew of any failers who were also bullies. The guards were a cautious breed of people. They preferred to talk about good, well-behaved students and not about poor students and ruffians. According to the picture they painted, all the children in their schools were excellent students. They were polite, had good manners, washed their hands every day, and some even washed their necks.

There were some ruffians, of course—if you could consider them ruffians, with one broken window a week and only two F's on their report cards.

At last the crocodile got lucky. He found the perfect boy in one of the schools. This boy loved to pick fights and got six failing grades a week! He was exactly what they were looking for. Gene wrote the boy's name and address on a piece of paper. Feeling pleased with himself, he hurried home.

Floptop wasn't as lucky.

He also found exactly the kind of boy they were looking for. A real treasure! Someone who'd had to repeat a grade. A bully. A truant. From a good family and who got eight failing grades a week. But this boy refused to have anything to do with anyone who got less than ten failing grades a week. And you couldn't find such a boy, even in your dreams. Floptop came home upset and went straight to bed.

chapter 12

School number 5.
DIMA.
He loves to start
fights!
He gets six failing
grades a week!
He hates
washing
himself!
He skips
school all
the time!

THE NEXT DAY THE grubby boy returned.

"Have you found someone yet?" he asked Gail, forgetting to say hello.

"Yes, we have," answered Gail. "I believe he's exactly what you wanted."

"He skips school all the time," said the crocodile.

"That's good!"

"He loves to start fights."

"Great!"

"And he gets six failing grades a week. Plus, he hates washing himself."

"Not enough F's," summed up their visitor, "but

the rest sounds good. Which school does he go to?"

"School number five," answered Gene.

"Five?" said the boy, somewhat surprised. "What's his name?"

"His name is Dima," said the crocodile, looking down at his notes. "He's exactly what you wanted!"

"What I wanted! What I wanted!" the boy shouted. "It's not at all what I wanted. That's *me* you're talking about. *I'm* Dima!" He was very upset.

"Did *you* find anyone?" the boy asked Floptop.

"Yes, I did," Floptop answered. "I found someone who gets eight F's. Only he doesn't want to be your friend because you get only six. He wants someone who gets ten F's. If you had ten F's, you'd get along just fine."

"No," said the boy. "Ten is too much. It's easier to get six." Slowly he headed for the door.

"Keep checking back," the crocodile shouted after him. "We'll find someone for you yet."

"I will!" said the boy, and he disappeared through the door.

chapter 13

ONE HOUR PASSED. Then another half hour. Suddenly the window opened and a strange-looking head with short horns and long floppy ears poked into the room.

"How do you do?" said the head. "I believe I have come to the right place."

"How do you do!" the friends answered.

They instantly recognized their visitor. Such a long neck could belong to only one animal—a giraffe.

"My name is Anita," said the guest. "I would like to make some friends."

She sniffed at the flowers on the window sill and continued, "You are all probably curious why such a charming and likable giraffe as I has no friends. Am I correct?"

Gene, Gail, and Floptop had to agree that this was so.

"In that case, I will explain it to you. My problem is that I am very tall. In order for someone to talk with me, they have to crane their neck way back." The giraffe stretched her neck and stared at herself in the mirror. "And when you have to walk down the street with your neck craned up, you are very likely to trip and fall into some hole or gutter! That's how I lost all my friends. A sad story, don't you agree?"

Gene, Gail, and Floptop had to agree that hers was a very sad story indeed.

The giraffe talked for a long time. Even so, she didn't say much. Finally, after a long discussion, Gene managed to get her to leave. The three friends all sighed in relief.

"Oh, well," said Gail, "it's time for us to go home, too."

They needed rest, after all.

chapter 14

UNFORTUNATELY, the crocodile didn't manage to get any rest. As soon as he got into bed someone knocked softly on the door.

When Gene opened the door, a small monkey wearing a lilac cap and a red sport suit appeared on the threshold.

"How do you do?" the crocodile said. "Please come in."

Without saying a word, the monkey walked inside and sat down in the visitors' chair.

"You came here looking for a friend, am I right?" Gene asked her.

The visitor nodded in agreement. She looked as if her mouth was stuffed with hot cereal or tennis balls.

Gene thought for a while, then asked her bluntly, "You probably don't know *how* to talk?"

The little monkey looked confused. If she nodded, it would mean, "Yes, I don't know how to talk." And if she shook her head, it would mean, "No, I don't know how to talk."

She had no choice but to open her mouth and empty out a collection of screws, bolts, boxes of shoe polish, keys, buttons, rubber bands, and all sorts of other interesting and useful articles.

"*I* know how to talk," she finally announced, and started to stuff the things back inside her cheeks.

"One minute!" the crocodile stopped her. "Why don't you first tell me what your name is and where you work?"

"Maria France," the monkey said. "I am a circus performer. I work with a trainer."

And she quickly began to stuff all her treasures back into her mouth.

"Well, what kind of a friend are you looking for?" Gene wanted to know.

The monkey thought for a while, then reached into her mouth to take out all the things that prevented her from talking.

"Wait!" Gene stopped her. "You are probably looking for a friend who doesn't like to talk very much. Am I right?"

"Right!" nodded the visitor. "Right, right, right!"

"In that case," said the crocodile, "why don't you check back with us in about a week."

After the monkey left, Gene went outside and wrote on the notice that was pinned by the entrance:

Then he thought for a while and added:

AND UNTIL MORNING

New surprises awaited Gene, however. When the monkey was stuffing all her treasures back into her mouth, she accidentally stuffed the crocodile's tiny alarm clock into her mouth as well. That's why Gene was late for work the next morning and had to have a serious discussion with the director of the zoo.

As for the monkey, after she left the crocodile, she became aware of a constant ticking in her ears. At six o'clock the next morning something rang so loudly inside her head that the poor monkey leaped out of her bed and hurried over to see Dr. Ivanov.

Dr. Ivanov examined her closely through his stethoscope and then pronounced, "One of two

63

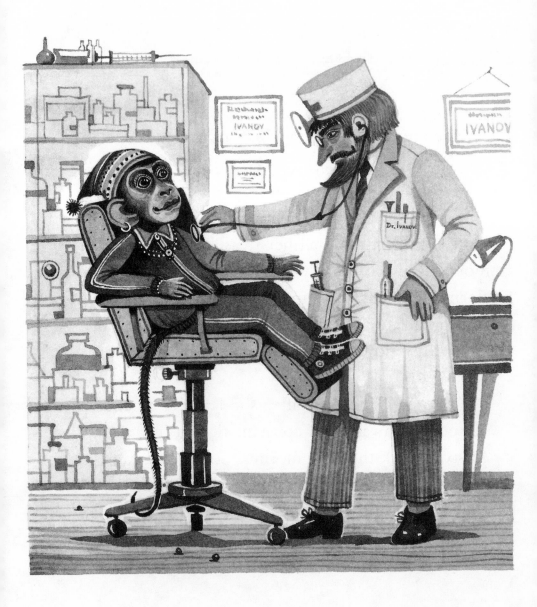

things is wrong: Either you have a nervous tic, or you have a disease unknown to science! In either case castor oil will cure it." He was very old-fashioned, this doctor, and didn't believe in modern medicines. "Tell me," he asked the monkey, "you're not experiencing this for the first time, am I right?"

Whichever way the monkey moved her head in response—yes or no—the answer came out that it wasn't for the first time. There was nothing else for her to do but take everything out of her mouth. Now the doctor understood.

"The next time you hear music," he said, "first check that you didn't stuff a radio inside your cheek—or the town clock."

On this note they parted.

chapter 15

SEVERAL EVENINGS later, Gene called a small meeting.

"What I want to say may not be very tactful," he began, "but I will say it anyway. I like what the three of us are doing very much. The House of Friendship was a great idea. But since we hatched this great idea, I have had no peace. Even at night, when all normal crocodiles are sleeping, I have to get up and greet visitors. It cannot go on like this! We have to come up with a solution."

"I think I've already found one," said Floptop, "but I'm afraid you are not going to like it!"

"What is it?"

"We have to build a new House of Friendship. It's as simple as that!"

"You are right," said Gene happily. "Then we can close down the old one."

"We'll close it only temporarily," Gail corrected him, "and later we will reopen in a new house!"

"And how are we going to do this?" asked Gene.

"First we have to find an empty lot," answered Gail. "Then we have to decide what materials we are going to use to build the house."

"Finding a lot is easy," said the crocodile. "There's a kindergarten behind my house, and next to it is a small empty lot. We can build it there!"

"What materials are we going to use?"

"Bricks, of course!"

"But where are we going to get them?"

"I don't know."

"I don't know either," said Gail.

"I don't know either," said Floptop.

"I have an idea!" Gail said suddenly. "Let's call directory assistance."

"Okay," agreed the crocodile, and picked up the telephone. "Hello, Information!" he said. "Could you please tell me where I can get bricks? We want to build a small house."

"One moment!" answered the operator. "Let me think. The name of the person in charge of bricks in our city is Ivan Ivanovich. You must get in touch with him."

"And where does he live?" asked Gene.

"He doesn't live," said the operator, "he works. In the tall building on the main square. Good-bye."

"That settles it," said Gene. "Let's go see Ivan Ivanovich." And he went to the closet and took out his best suit.

chapter 16

VAN IVANOVICH SAT behind his desk in his spacious office, immersed in work.

He took a piece of paper from a tall stack of papers, wrote PERMISSION GRANTED, IVAN IVANOVICH, and placed it on his left.

Then he took the next piece of paper, wrote NOT GRANTED, IVAN IVANOVICH, and placed it on his right.

And so on...

GRANTED, IVAN IVANOVICH.

NOT GRANTED, IVAN IVANOVICH.

"How do you do?" the friends greeted him politely as they entered the room.

"How do you do?" answered Ivan Ivanovich without stopping his work.

Gene took off his new hat and put it down on the edge of the desk. Then and there Ivan Ivanovich wrote GRANTED, IVAN IVANOVICH on the brim because he had just finished writing NOT GRANTED, IVAN IVANOVICH on a piece of paper.

"We are here because we need bricks," Gail started.

"How many?" Ivan Ivanovich wanted to know. He continued to write.

"Many," Floptop put in hurriedly.

"No," answered Ivan Ivanovich, "I can't give you many. I can only give you half of that."

"Why is that?"

"That's my policy," explained Ivan Ivanovich. "I grant only half."

"But why do you have such a policy?" asked Floptop.

"Very simple," said Ivan Ivanovich. "If I agree to everything, and if I grant everything to everyone, then they will say I'm too generous and anyone can get anything they want out of me. On the other hand, if I don't grant anything to anyone, then they will say I am useless and only get in everyone's way. This way, nobody can say anything bad about me. Do you understand?"

"Yes, we understand," said the visitors.

"So how many bricks do you need?"

"We wanted to build two small houses," said the cunning crocodile.

"Well, then," said Ivan Ivanovich, "in that case I will give you enough bricks for one small house. That will be one thousand bricks. Agreed?"

"Agreed!" Gail nodded. "We also need a truck to transport the bricks."

"That is not possible," said Ivan Ivanovich. "I cannot give you a truck. I can only give you a half-truck."

"But half a truck will not be able to move," argued Floptop.

"True," agreed the head of the brick department. "It won't be able to move. In that case we will do it this way. I will give you a whole truck, but it will deliver the bricks only halfway."

"That will take it as far as the kindergarten," said the cunning Gene.

"We are in agreement then," replied Ivan Ivanovich.

And he went back to his important work, taking a piece of paper from the pile, writing GRANTED, IVAN IVANOVICH, and reaching for the next piece of paper.

chapter 17

THE FOLLOWING DAY a large truck pulled up next to the kindergarten, and two workers unloaded one thousand bricks.

"We have to put a fence around our lot," said Gail, "so no one will bother us when we start building."

"You are right," agreed Gene. "We will do that first!"

They found some wooden boards, planted poles in the four corners of the lot, and put up a low wooden fence. Then the real work began.

Floptop and Gail brought mud while the croco-dile put on a canvas apron and became the brick-layer.

One thing worried Gene.

"You know," he said to Floptop, "if any of my friends see me they will say, 'Isn't it a shame about Crocodile Gene having to do such menial labor!' It will be very embarrassing!"

"Why don't you wear a mask?" suggested Floptop. "Then no one will recognize you!"

"You're right!" The crocodile hit himself on the head. "Why didn't I think of that!"

From then on he wore a mask to work on the house. Nobody recognized the crocodile behind the mask, except once, when the fat crocodile Val from the zoo passed by. He cried, "Ho-ho! What do I see! Crocodile Gene is working on construction! How are things with you?"

"Things are just fine," answered Gene in a strange voice. "Only I am not Gene, number one, and number two, I am not a crocodile."

That took care of Val!

chapter 18

IT HAPPENED THAT one day Gene was the first to arrive at the construction site. Written along the fence he saw the following message:

"Well, I never!" Gene said to himself. "I wonder who could have brought it here? Floptop, perhaps? He has a lot of strange friends!"

The crocodile sat down to wait for Floptop.

He came along half an hour later, humming a song.

"Do you by any chance know how a dog got here?" the crocodile asked.

Floptop opened his eyes wide.

"No, I don't," he said. "The dog wasn't here yesterday. Maybe Gail brought it here?"

But when Gail arrived, it turned out that she hadn't brought any nasty dog either.

"That means the dog came here by itself," said Floptop.

"By itself?" exclaimed the crocodile. "In that case, would you mind telling me who is responsible for the writing on the fence?"

"The dog, of course. So nobody would bother it."

"Whoever is responsible doesn't matter," decided the girl. "What we have to do is lure the dog out of there. Let's tie a piece of sausage to a string and throw it over the fence. When the dog grabs the sausage in its teeth, we'll pull it out through the gate."

And that's what they did. They took a piece of sausage from Floptop's supper, tied it to a string, and threw it over the fence.

But nobody pulled at the string.

"Maybe it doesn't like sausage," said Floptop. "Maybe it likes canned fish. Or cheese sandwiches."

"If I weren't wearing new trousers," said Gene, "I would show it a thing or two!"

It's impossible to guess how this whole thing would have ended if a cat hadn't suddenly popped up from behind the fence. In her mouth was the piece of sausage on the string.

The cat looked at the three friends and scooted off as fast as her legs could carry her. So quickly that Floptop didn't have a chance to pull at the string and grab his supper back.

"What is this?" he said, sounding very disappointed. "They write one thing and do something else entirely!" He went through the gate. "There's no dog here!"

"And there never was one!" said Gail. "Someone decided to play a trick on us! That's all!"

"I bet I know who!" cried Gene. "It's that old woman, Fedora! It couldn't be anyone else! Because of her we haven't done any work yet today. And tomorrow she'll think up something else. Mark my words!"

"Tomorrow she won't get a chance to think up anything else," Floptop announced firmly. He wiped the words off the fence and wrote in their place: BEWARE: A NASTY FLOPTOP!

Then he picked out a long, heavy wooden pole and propped it on top of the gate. Now if anyone tried to open the gate and stick their curious nose inside, the pole would instantly bang them over the head.

Then Gail, Gene, and Floptop climbed over the fence and went their separate ways.

chapter 19

LATE EVERY EVENING the old woman Fedora left her house to do night mischief. She drew mustaches on posters and placards, dumped garbage out of garbage cans, and sometimes shot at strollers with her toy pistol, just to frighten them.

That evening she and her pet rat, Laura, headed for downtown. She had decided to go to the construction site of the new building first. She wanted to make a real mess there.

When the old woman came to the fence, she saw the sign:

Interesting, thought the old woman. I wonder who this nasty Floptop is? I have to find out!

She was dying to open the gate and look inside. But as soon as she did, the pole that was propped on top of it fell and hit her painfully on the nose.

"Hooligans!" screamed the old woman. "Scoundrels! I'll get even with you. You'll be sorry!" And tucking her pet rat under her arm, she headed for the zoo.

A menacing plan of revenge was already taking shape in Fedora's head. She knew that a mean and stupid rhinoceros named Fledgling lived in the zoo. On Sundays the old woman fed him bagels, trying to teach him to obey her. The rhinoceros ate five whole bagels, and Fedora was convinced he was now completely tame. She wanted to order him to run to the construction site to punish this nasty Floptop and shatter everything in sight.

The gates to the zoo were locked, but the old woman jumped over the fence and headed for the cage where the rhinoceros lived.

The rhinoceros was sound asleep, of course. In his sleep he snored, of course. And he snored so loudly that it was hard to understand how he could sleep with so much noise.

"Hey, you, get up!" the old woman shouted. "There's work to do!"

But Fledgling didn't hear a thing.

She started punching his side through the bars of his cage. This didn't get any results either.

The old woman had no choice but to search for

a long stick and beat the rhinoceros's back with it.

Finally Fledgling woke up, furious at being disturbed. He no longer remembered any bagels.

Fedora opened the door of his cage, crying, "Charge! On the double!" Then she ran to the zoo's exit.

The rhinoceros charged after her, and not because she ordered him to. He just wanted to butt this nasty old hag.

Fedora came to a stop right in front of the gate.

"Stop!" she said. "I have to open the gates."

But the rhinoceros did not stop. He rushed headlong at the old woman and butted her so hard that she flew over the fence.

"Scoundrel! Hooligan!" shouted the old woman, rubbing her sore parts. "I will show you who's boss!"

But she didn't have a chance to show him any-

thing. The rhinoceros broke through the gates and charged after her again.

"You stupid moron!" cried Fedora as she ran. "I'll run to the police! They'll give you what-for! They'll teach you a lesson!"

But she couldn't run to the police. Most likely they would have taught *her* a lesson and not the rhinoceros.

It's hard to say what would have happened next if there hadn't been a tall tree on the road. It took the old woman just ten seconds to climb to the very top of that tree.

"Saved!" she said, settling comfortably in the branches. "There is no way he can climb up here. Koo-koo!"

The rhinoceros stomped the ground for a while, then found himself a suitable ditch nearby and lay down to sleep.

chapter 20

JUST AS THE RHI-
NOCEROS fell asleep,
Floptop, after spending
the whole evening with
the crocodile, decided
to head for home. On
the way he decided to
stop by the construction site to make sure everything was in order.

Floptop walked slowly down the dark street.

Everyone in the city had gone to sleep a long time ago, and there was not a soul around. Suddenly Floptop heard a rustling noise! It seemed to come from the top of the tree right in front of him.

"Who's there?" he asked.

"It's me," answered a familiar voice. "Fedora."

And Floptop indeed recognized his old enemy in the tree's branches.

"What are you doing up there?"

"Hanging," answered the old woman. "For two whole hours."

"I see," said Floptop, and continued on his way.

He wasn't surprised by Fedora's answer. If she felt like hanging from a tree for two hours, that was her own business. Still, Floptop went back.

"I'm curious. How long did it take you to get up there? At least an hour, I bet."

"Really!" said the old woman indignantly. "Do you take me for a snail? It took me only ten seconds to climb up here!"

"Ten seconds! Is that all? But why?"

"Because the rhinoceros was chasing me. That's why!"

"Wow!" exclaimed Floptop. "But who let him out of the zoo? And why?"

But the old woman didn't want to explain anything more to him.

"The more you know, the older you get!" was all she would say.

Floptop had heard a lot about this vicious and stupid rhinoceros and he knew that something had to be done about him. Otherwise, not only Fedora but other people in the city would wind up like Christmas tree ornaments.

I must find him, decided Floptop.

In a few seconds he stumbled on the rhinoceros, who gave a loud howl and hurled himself after little Floptop. They raced along the street with the speed of lightning. Finally Floptop turned a corner while the rhinoceros charged straight ahead.

Now Floptop was running *after* the rhinoceros, trying to keep up with him. At the first opportunity he meant to call the zoo and ask them to send help.

I wonder how they will reward me for his capture? he thought as he ran. He knew there were three kinds of medals: For Rescuing the Drowning, For Bravery, and For Effort. Rescuing the Drowning didn't fit at all.

They will probably give me a medal for bravery, he decided, still chasing after Fledgling.

No, they probably won't give it to me for bravery, flickered through his head when he found himself running again from the enraged rhinoceros.

After running around the city for twenty-two miles he was convinced that he would get the medal for effort.

Then Floptop noticed a small house standing apart from other houses and instantly headed toward it. The rhinoceros was close behind him. They ran around the house five or six times.

Now you couldn't tell who was chasing whom. Was the rhinoceros chasing Floptop, was Floptop running after the rhinoceros, or was each running by himself?

Floptop jumped to the side to try and figure things out, while the rhinoceros continued to run around the house in circles. Floptop sat quietly on a bench and thought about it.

Suddenly a brilliant idea came into his head.

"Hey, friend!" he shouted to the rhinoceros. "Follow me!" And he ran down a long, gradually narrowing lane.

Fledgling charged after him.

The lane got narrower and narrower. Finally it got so narrow that the rhinoceros couldn't go any farther. He was stuck between the houses like a cork in a bottle.

In the morning the zookeepers came. They thanked Floptop for a long time and even promised to give him a live baby elephant when they had an extra one.

It took the entire fire department to get old Fedora down from the tree that day.

chapter 21

OW THERE WAS no one to interfere with the construction, but it was still progressing very slowly.

"If the three of us continue to work alone," Gene said one day, "it will take us at least a year to finish our house! We desperately need assistants!"

"You're right," agreed Floptop. "And I even know where we can get them."

"Where?"

"Don't rush me. I'm going to tell you. Now, who are we building the house for?"

"For anyone who wants a friend."

"Well, then, *they* should help us! Right?"

"Right!" cried Gene.

Gail added, "That was good thinking on your part! We will ask them to help us."

From then on the work progressed at a much quicker pace. The giraffe Anita came, the monkey Maria France, and, of course, Dima. Also a very well mannered little girl named Mary joined the construction crew. Mary, an honor student, didn't have any friends because she was shy and not very noticeable. Nobody even noticed when she first appeared and started helping with the construction of the house.

The builders worked late into the night. When it got dark, the giraffe took a lantern in her mouth and lit up the construction site. They couldn't thank her for this, because if anyone did she would say "You are welcome," and the lantern would fall on their head.

One evening a tall red-haired man with a notepad in his hand came to the site, drawn there by the light.

"How are you!" he said. "I'm from a newspaper.

Would you explain to me, please, what you are doing here?"

"We are building a house," answered Gene.

"What kind of house? For what purpose?" the reporter asked. "I am interested in figures."

"Our house will be small," the crocodile explained to him. "Five paces in width and five paces in length."

"And how many floors?"

"One floor."

"Check," said the reporter, and scribbled something on his pad. The giraffe was holding the lantern for him so he could see what he was doing.

"Check. What else?"

"The house will have four windows and one door," continued Gene. "It will not be too high— only seven feet. Anyone who wants a friend will be able to come to us and choose one. Right here by the window we will put a worktable, and here, by the door, a couch for visitors."

"And who is working on the construction?"

"All of us," said Gene. "Me, Floptop, the giraffe, Dima, and others."

"That makes perfect sense," said the reporter, "but your figures are not very interesting. I will have to make some corrections." And he headed for the gate. "Good-bye! Read tomorrow's paper!"

The next morning the friends read the following article in the paper.

NEWS

A wonderful house is being constructed in our city:
THE HOUSE OF FRIENDSHIP.
Its height —10 floors.
Width — 50 paces. Length — same.

The construction crew consists of
ten crocodiles, ten giraffes, ten monkeys, and
ten honor students.
The House of Friendship will be finished on
schedule.

"Well!" said the ten crocodiles after they had read the article. "Those are some corrections!"

"He is full of hot air," the ten honor students said bluntly. "We have met his kind before!"

And the builders unanimously agreed not to allow the tall red-headed man to come near their house again. Even for a twenty-six-gun salute!

chapter 22

THE HOUSE GREW by leaps and bounds. At first it only reached to the crocodile's knee. Then his neck. Then it covered him completely. Nearly everyone was happy. Only Floptop grew sadder and sadder each day.

"What is the matter with you?" the crocodile finally asked him. "Are you worried about something?"

"Yes," answered Floptop, "I am very worried. They are thinking of closing our store. Nobody is buying secondhand merchandise anymore."

"Why didn't you say something before?" asked Gene.

"I didn't want to bother you with trifles. You have enough troubles of your own!"

"Some trifles!" exclaimed the crocodile. "Don't worry. Everything will be all right. We'll think of something."

"I've got it!" he cried after five minutes. "What time does your store open?"

"At eleven."

"Good! Everything will be fine!"

The first thing the crocodile did the next morning was to excuse himself from work. The fat crocodile Val took over for him at the zoo.

Gene and the other friends who were free that morning met at the entrance to Floptop's store two hours before it opened. They milled around near the entrance, looking in the windows and exclaiming impatiently, "When are they going to open up?

When are they going to open up?"

The store manager and the salesclerks came. They too started looking in the windows of their store and exclaiming, "When are they going to open up? When are they going to open up?"

Old Fedora passed by with her pet rat, Laura. She thought for a while and then joined the line.

A little old man carrying a big bag came up to her and asked what was going to be on sale. Fedora did not say anything. She only shrugged meaningfully.

Probably something very interesting, decided the old man, and also peeked in the windows.

By eleven o'clock the line had reached catastrophic proportions.

When the doors opened, a mob of people burst into the store and bought everything they could lay their hands on. The only things that nobody wanted were kerosene lamps. They all had electricity at home.

So the store manager got out colored markers and wrote:

WE HAVE KEROSENE LAMPS!
ON SALE OUTSIDE.
ONLY TWO TO A CUSTOMER!

Instantly all the shoppers headed outside and started grabbing the lamps. Those who managed to buy them were very pleased with themselves, and those who didn't get the lamps became upset and blamed the store's management.

As for old Fedora, she managed to acquire two sets of lamps—one for herself and one for her Laura. And she still has those lamps. As the saying goes, for a rainy day.

chapter 23

ONE SUNDAY, Gene turned to his assistants and said, "The walls of the house are almost finished. Now we have to decide what material to use for the roof."

"What do you mean, what material?" cried the giraffe. "That is obvious!" She bent down to straighten a brick that lay crooked on the wall and continued, "The roof is usually made out of something waterproof! However, we don't really need a roof."

"Thank you," the crocodile said to Anita. "That was a big help. And what does our dear monkey have to say about this?"

Maria France thought about it for a moment, then took a clean handkerchief out of her pocket, emptied her belongings onto it, and said, "Nothing."

And she carefully put her treasures back into her mouth.

Lately the monkey's cheeks had grown noticeably fatter. That was because her new friends had started giving her all kinds of small articles for safekeeping.

"Well," continued Gene, "doesn't anyone have any ideas?"

"Can I say something?" asked the quiet little girl, Mary. "I think I have a solution. We have a fence around our house. And we don't really need it anymore. We could make the roof out of it."

"Hooray!" cried the builders. "She has found the perfect solution!"

"I agree," said Gene, "but in that case we need nails." He added up the number in his head. "About forty nails! But where are we going to get them?"

Everyone looked at Floptop.

"If we need them, then we need them!" he said modestly. "I will get the nails!"

He thought awhile and then ran to the edge of the city, to the main construction warehouse.

At the warehouse gates the head watchman sat on a bench, wearing warm winter boots and smoking a cigarette.

Floptop started the conversation from a distance.

"The sun is shining, the grass is green," he said, "and we need nails so desperately. Won't you give us a few?"

"It's not the grass that is green," answered the watchman. "Someone spilled paint. And there are no nails. Every carton has to be accounted for."

"But the birds are singing," continued Floptop. "Spellbinding! Maybe you could find some spare ones. We don't need many."

The sign reads:

THE MAIN
CONSTRUCTION
WAREHOUSE

"If only the birds did the singing," the watch-man said with a sigh, "but it's the gates that are squeaking. And I am not going to look! There is nothing extra here!"

"That's a shame," said Floptop, "that it's not the

birds that do the squeaking. Because we are building a house of friendship!"

"A house of friendship?" The watchman became interested. "That is a different kettle of fish. I will give you the nails. Take them. But I will have to give you bent nails. Okay?"

"Okay," said Floptop happily. "Thank you very much. But in that case, would you also give me a bent hammer?"

"A bent hammer?" asked the surprised watchman. "Whatever for?"

"What do you mean, whatever for? To hammer down the bent nails!"

Here the booted watchman, who had heard a lot of strange things in his life, couldn't stop himself from roaring with laughter.

"All right, you win. I will give you straight nails. And I will straighten out the bent nails myself."

The happy Floptop ran back to the construction site.

chapter 24

T LAST THE HOUSE
was almost finished. It
only needed to be
painted inside and out.
And here the friends
had a difference of
opinion.

Crocodile Gene,
who was green, was convinced that the house
should be painted green, because this color was

most pleasing to the eye. The brown monkey Maria France felt that brown was the most pleasing color. And the lanky Anita insisted that giraffe color was the nicest.

Finally Floptop suggested that each of them take one wall and paint it any color they wanted.

The finished house looked beautiful. Each wall was a different color—one green, one brown, and the third yellow with black spots. The fourth wall sparkled with all the colors of the rainbow. Dima had painted it. He didn't have a favorite color, so he had run to all the neighbors' houses, dipping his brush into every paint bucket in the city.

"You know," Gail said to Floptop, "Gene and I decided that you should give the welcoming speech at the opening of our house."

"But I'm scared that I won't be any good," answered Floptop. "I've never given a speech before!"

"Don't be scared. You'll do just fine," Gail reassured him. "All you need to do is practice a little.

I'll give you a short poem, and you can walk around and repeat it again and again. If you can recite it without stumbling, you'll be able to give any speech."

And she told him a sharp tongue twister.

"How much dew
would a dewdrop drop
if a dewdrop did drop dew
in the morning?"

That's a very easy poem, decided Floptop. I can repeat it without practice. And he began to recite:

"How much dew
would a dewdrop drip
if dropdue dropped
in the morning?"

No, he thought, I'm not saying it right. Why "dewdrop drip" and why "dropdue dropped?" The right words are "dewdrop drop" and "dewdrop did drop." Okay, let me start from the beginning.

"How much dew…"

he began correctly.

"Would a dewdrop prop…"

was *almost* right. But then he came out with:

"If a dude dropped dip
in the morning?"

"What's going on?" Floptop got angry at himself. "I can't put two worlds together! That means I
have to plactish more."

And he plactished and plactished all night.

chapter 25

THE OPENING WAS a huge success. All the builders came feeling happy and dressed in their best clothes.

Crocodile Gene wore his best suit and his best straw hat. Gail wore her favorite red hood. And the giraffe Anita and the monkey Maria France looked as if they had just come from the dry cleaner's.

Gail, Gene, and Floptop came to the front door together.

"Dear gentlemen," Gail started first.

"Dear ladies," continued the crocodile.

"And our dear little ladies and gentlemen," Floptop piped up just to say something too.

"Now Floptop is going to make a speech!" said Gail.

Floptop trembled with nervousness.

"Go on." The crocodile nudged Floptop.

"Certainly," answered Floptop, suddenly tripping over his words. "I plactished all light!"

And Floptop made his speech. Here is Floptop's speech:

> "Well, what can a shay? All of ush are wery happy.
> We beat and beat and finally we finissed!
> Hurry for us! Hooray!"

"Hooray!" shouted the builders.

"Bell?" asked Floptop. "Wasn't I bellific?"

"Bellific!" Gene praised him. "You're a real trouper!"

Then the crocodile proudly cut the ribbon that was stretched across the entrance, and Floptop opened the front door to the sound of loud applause.

But as soon as Floptop opened the front door, a heavy red brick fell on him! Everything in his head began to swim. He no longer knew where the sky was, or the ground, or the house, or where he, Floptop, was.

Still, Floptop realized immediately who put the brick on top of the door.

"You just wait!" he said. "Just wait, you miserable Fedora! I'll get even with you yet!"

The miserable Fedora was standing on her balcony watching through a telescope the huge bump that was growing on the top of Floptop's head.

She let her pet rat, Laura, look through the telescope too. Both were happy as never before.

chapter 26

"N OW WE HAVE TO get down to business," said Gail to her listeners. "We'll write the name of everyone who is looking for a friend in the book.

Who wants to go first, please?"

There was silence.

"Who's going to go first?" Gail asked again.

"Isn't there anyone who wants to go first?"

Everyone kept quiet. So Gail turned to the long-legged giraffe. "Don't *you* want a friend?"

"No," answered Anita. "I already have a friend."

"And who is that?" asked Floptop.

"What do you mean, who? The monkey, of course! We became friends a long time ago."

"But how do you walk together?" asked Floptop. "I mean, she can fall into a deep hole or something!"

"No, she cannot," said the giraffe. She bent down, bit off a piece of the crocodile's hat, and continued, "When we take a walk, she sits on my neck like a collar. We find it very comfortable, and we can talk!"

"Isn't that something!" said Floptop, amazed. "I would never have thought of that!"

"How about you, Dima?" asked Gail. "Have you found yourself a friend?"

"I have," answered Dima, "and what a friend!"

"Who is it, if it's not a secret? We'd like to meet him."

"This is who." Dima pointed at Mary.

"But she doesn't get failing grades," said the surprised crocodile.

"That is bad," agreed the boy, "but failing grades are not the most important thing in life. If a person doesn't have any failing grades, that doesn't mean he's not worth anything. I can copy off her, and besides, she helps me do my homework! So there!"

"In that case," said Gail, "I wish you both the best! We are all happy for you. Am I right?"

"Right!" agreed Gene and Floptop. "But who are we going to find friends for if everyone has already found a friend without our help?"

That was a good question. There was no one who wanted a friend.

"What is happening?" Floptop said sadly. "We worked and worked to build the house and all for nothing!"

"Not for nothing," Gail disagreed. "First of all, we introduced the giraffe to the monkey. Right?"

"Right!" everyone cried.

"In the second place, we introduced Dima and Mary. Right?"

"Right!"

"And in the third place, we now have a new

house and we can give it to someone as a present. To Floptop, for instance, who lives in a telephone booth. Am I right?"

"You're right!" everyone cried out for the third time.

"No, you are not right," Floptop said suddenly. "We have to give this house not to me but to all of us. We'll make it into a club and we will meet here in the evenings to play and to see one another!"

"But what about you?" asked the crocodile. "Are you going to continue to live in the telephone booth?"

"It's okay," answered Floptop. "I'll manage somehow. But if only someone would offer me a job as a toy in a kindergarten, it would make me very, very happy. During the day I would play with the children, and at night I could sleep there and guard it."

"We will all go to the kindergarten and ask them to give you a job," the animals told Floptop. "Any kindergarten would be more than happy to hire you."

"Do you really mean it?" asked Floptop. "Then I am very happy."

118

And that is exactly what they did. They made the house into a club and gave Floptop to the kindergarten next door as a toy. Everyone was very happy!

That is why I decided to take a pencil in my hand and write two short words:

THE END

But as soon as I picked up the pencil and wrote down the words "the end," Floptop came up to me.

"What do you mean, the end?" he cried. "You can't write 'the end'! I still haven't gotten even with the mean Fedora! First I have to get even, and then you can write 'the end.'"

"Well, in that case, get even," I said. "I'll be curious to see how it's going to turn out."

"Very simple," answered Floptop. "You will see!"

Everything turned out very simple indeed.

The very next morning Gene, Gail, and Floptop marched over to see old Fedora. In their hands they held big beautiful brightly colored balloons.

Fedora was sitting on a bench plotting all sorts of mean tricks.

"Would you like a balloon?" Floptop offered her.

"For free?"

"Of course for free!"

"Give it to me," said the old woman, and grabbed all of Floptop's brightly colored balloons. "Finders keepers, losers weepers," she announced.

"Would you like some more?" asked Gail.

"Give them to me!"

Now the old woman was holding two bunches of balloons in her hands, and they were lifting her off the ground.

"How about some more?" Gene asked, offering her his balloons.

"Absolutely!"

Now Gene's balloons were in the greedy old woman's hands, too.

Now not two but three bunches of balloons were lifting Fedora off the ground. Slowly, very slowly, she was rising up and floating toward the clouds.

"I don't want to go into the sky!" she shouted.

But it was too late. The wind lifted her up and carried her farther and farther.

"Hooligans!" she shrieked. "I will be back! I will get even with you for this! I don't want to go away!"

"What if she does come back?" Gail asked Floptop. "Then she will definitely make our lives miserable."

"Don't worry," said Floptop. He called out to the old woman, "You can come back when you're ready to be our friend." Then he turned to his friends. "The wind will carry her so far away that unless someone helps her, she will never come back. If she continues to be mean and rotten, nobody will even think of helping her. But if she comes back, we'll know we've taught her a lesson."

"We sure will," said the crocodile.

"We sure will," agreed Gail.

After that, there was nothing else for me to do but take my pencil and write five short words:

THE END OF THE TALE

Eduard Uspensky is Russia's best-known children's book author. His works have been published throughout Europe and Asia and have inspired more than thirty films and ten plays. He is the author of *Uncle Fedya, His Dog, and His Cat*, which *School Library Journal* called "perfectly suited to the imaginative and comic sense of young children," and *The Little Warranty People*. He is the publisher of a children's magazine and currently works with young writers in Russia, where he lives.

Vladimir Shpitalnik studied at the Moscow Art Theatre School and received his M.F.A. degree from the Yale School of Drama. He has designed many theatrical productions in both Russia and the United States. He is the illustrator of *Uncle Fedya, His Dog, and His Cat* and *The Little Warranty People* as well as other children's books published in Russia. He lives in New Haven, Connecticut with his wife, Connie Evans.